KU-016-057

Contents

A Note About the Author

James Fenimore Cooper was born in New Jersey, North America on 15th September 1789. His family lived on a farm in Cooperstown, in the north of New York State.

Cooper had five brothers and seven sisters. He went to school at Yale. But he did not behave well and he had to leave. In 1805, Cooper became a sailor. He was in the US Navy until 1810. In 1811 Cooper's father died. Cooper married Susan De Lancey and they lived on the farm. From 1812 to 1821 Cooper worked very hard. But he was poor. He gave a lot of money to his brothers and sisters. In 1820, he started to write stories. Cooper's adventure stories were about life in the forests and the wild lands of North America.

The Last of the Mohicans was Cooper's most popular story. Many people liked the adventures of Hawk-eye. Cooper became rich and he travelled to Europe.

Cooper wrote five stories about Hawk-eye: *The Pioneers* (1823), *The Last of the Mohicans* (1826), *The Pathfinder* (1840) and *The Deerslayer* (1841). He also wrote *The Spy* (1821), *The Pilot* (1823) and *The Prairie* (1827). James Fenimore Cooper died on 14th September 1851.

A Note About This Story

Place: Lake Horican on the Hudson River. The author gave this name to Lake George. (Look at the map.) It is in the east of North America. Today, the area is called New York State. At the time of this story, North America was not independent. North America became independent from Europe in 1787.

Time: 1757. Armies from England and France are fighting in North America. Both countries want the land.

———

The Indian people had lived in the land for thousands of years. They got their food from the land. They caught fish in the rivers and lakes. They hunted deer, bears and birds in the forests. They ate the meat from these animals. They made clothes from the animals' skins.

There were many different Indian tribes, or families. These are some of the tribes who lived near the Hudson River:

Mohawks	'mɔʊhɔːks	*Delawares*	'deləweəz
Lenni-Lenape	leni 'lenɑːpeɪ	*Hurons*	'hʊəronz
Oneidas	ɒ'naɪdæs	*Mengwe*	'meŋgweɪ
Senecas	'seneɪkæs	*Iroquois*	'ɪrəkwɔɪ
Mohicans	mə'hiːkənz	*Mingoes*	'mɪŋgəʊz

In 1607, English people came to North America. In 1608, French people came. They hunted the animals.

They took the soft animals' skins to Europe.

Soon more and more Europeans came. They wanted the Indians' land. The kings of France and England sent soldiers to North America. The soldiers built strong forts to live in. The soldiers brought guns. The Indians fought for the armies from England and France. In this story, the Hurons are fighting for the French. The Mohawks are fighting for the English.

a fort

a waterfall

a canoe   a paddle

a hunting-gun

a meeting house

a necklace

a knife

a deer   a bear   a cave

Note: St = Saint (e.g. St Lawrence)

The People in This Story

Cora Munro
ˌkɔːrə mʌnˈrəʉ

Alice Munro
ˈælɪs mʌnˈrəʉ

General Munro
ˈdʒenrəl mʌnˈrəʉ

General Webb
ˈdʒenrəl ˈweb

Magua
ˈmægwə

Hawk-eye
ˈhɔːkaɪ

Chingachgook
tʃɪnˈgætʃgʊk

Uncas
ˈʊnkæs

General Montcalm
ˈdʒenrəl mɒnˈkɑːm

Tamenund
tæmenʊnd

Duncan Heyward
ˈdʌnkʌn heɪwʊd

7

1

The Two Sisters

It was the year 1757. The place was the dangerous and wild land, west of the Hudson River. It was the third year of the war in North America. The war was between England and France. Each country wanted the land for itself.

Indian tribes had always lived in that land. In the war, some tribes were fighting for the French. Other tribes were fighting for the English.

——

Fort Edward was on the Hudson River. General Webb was the commander of the English army at Fort Edward. He was waiting for news of General Montcalm. Montcalm was the commander of the French army.

The news came one morning. An Indian called Magua arrived.

'Montcalm and the French army are coming towards Fort William Henry,' Magua told General Webb.

Fort William Henry was fifteen miles away. It was at the south end of Lake Horican.

'How many men has Montcalm got?' asked Webb.

'As many as the leaves on the trees,' said Magua. 'General Munro wants more soldiers at Fort William Henry.'

'I will send fifteen hundred men,' said General Webb.

General Munro was the commander of the English army at Fort William Henry. He had two daughters – Cora and Alice. Cora was about twenty-three years old and Alice was eighteen. Cora had dark hair and a beautiful face. Alice had fair hair and blue eyes.

These two young women were at Fort Edward. But they were going to travel to Fort William Henry. They were going to meet their father.

General Webb spoke to Cora and Alice.

'Magua knows a secret path through the forest,' said General Webb. 'He will be your guide. Magua and Major Duncan Heyward will take you to Fort William Henry.'

Major Duncan Heyward was a young English officer. He and the two young women left Fort Edward. They rode on horses. Magua walked in front of them. Alice watched Magua.

'I don't like him, Cora,' she said. 'What do you think? Will we be safe in the forest with Magua?'

'We must trust Magua,' said Cora.

'The French know our soldiers' paths,' said Duncan. 'But Magua's path is secret.' He smiled at Alice, and she smiled at him. Duncan Heyward was in love with Alice.

'Magua is a Huron,' said Duncan. 'But he lived with the Mohawks. The Mohawks are friends of the English. Magua came to us. Your father—' Duncan stopped.

Then he said, 'But I don't remember all the story.'

Duncan knew more about Magua. But he did not tell Cora and Alice. He did not say, 'A few years ago, your father's men beat Magua. Now Magua hates your father.' Duncan did not want to frighten the young women.

So they followed Magua through the forest.

2

Lost in the Forest

A few miles west of Fort Edward, three men were sitting near a river. Two of the men were Indians. The other man was a white man. Chingachgook and his son, Uncas, were Mohicans. The white man was a scout called Hawk-eye. Hawk-eye had a long hunting-gun.

The three men were talking.

'My tribe is the oldest Indian tribe,' Chingachgook said. 'The blood of the Mohican chiefs is in me. Many summers ago, my tribe came here to the land of the Delawares.'

'Where are the Mohicans now?' asked Hawk-eye.

'Where are the flowers of those summers?' said Chingachgook. 'Gone. All dead. After my death, Uncas will be the last of the Mohicans.'

Suddenly, they heard a noise. They turned quickly. Hawk-eye lifted his gun. 'Who is it?' he said.

Duncan Heyward rode out of the forest. Cora and Alice followed him.

'I am an English officer,' Duncan said. 'We have come from Fort Edward. How far is it to Fort William Henry?'

Hawk-eye laughed. 'Fort William Henry? You are going the wrong way,' he said. 'You are near Glenn's Falls.'

'The wrong way!' said Duncan. 'Then we are lost. But our Indian guide—'

'You have an Indian guide but you are lost in the forest?' said Hawk-eye. 'That is very strange. Is he a Delaware?'

'He is called Magua. He is a Huron,' said Duncan. 'But he lives with the Mohawks, and he is a guide for the Eng—'

'A Huron!' said Hawk-eye quickly. 'You can trust a Mohican or a Delaware. But you cannot trust a Huron! Your guide will lead you to his friends. They will kill you. Let me see him.'

Magua was standing behind Cora's horse. Hawk-eye looked at him. Then he went and spoke to Chingachgook and Uncas.

Magua moved quickly. He ran into the forest.

Hawk-eye, Chingachgook and Uncas ran after him. But Magua escaped.

'What can I do?' thought Duncan. 'We are lost.'

He turned to Hawk-eye. 'Will you take us to Fort William Henry?' he asked. 'We will give you money.'

Hawk-eye looked at Cora and Alice. 'We will take you,' he told Duncan. 'Money is not important. We will not leave you and the two young women here. Magua and his Huron friends will find you. Come now – quickly!'

Duncan and Hawk-eye spoke to Cora and Alice. The sisters got off their horses. The Mohicans took the animals away.

'They will hide the horses until the morning,' said Hawk-eye. He pulled a canoe from the tall grass at the side of the river. 'Get into the canoe,' he said. 'We will go to a cave and we will stay there tonight.'

Duncan, Cora and Alice got into the canoe. Hawk-eye pushed the canoe to the middle of the river. Then he got into the canoe. He started to paddle along the river. Soon they heard the sound of a great waterfall in front of them – Glenn's Falls.

A few minutes later, they saw the waterfall.

Alice was afraid. She closed her eyes.

A few minutes later, Hawk-eye came back with Chingachgook and Uncas. The scout led everybody to a cave behind the waterfall. The cave was deep and narrow and dark. Hawk-eye immediately made a fire.

Alice looked at the tall young Mohican, Uncas.

'A strong man is guarding us,' she said quietly to her sister. 'We will be safe tonight.'

3

The Fight at Glenn's Falls

Hawk-eye woke Duncan early the next morning.

'We must go,' he said. 'I will get the canoe. Wake Miss Cora and Miss Alice. But do not make any noise.'

Duncan went to the back of the cave. 'Cora. Alice,' he said quietly. 'Wake up.'

Suddenly there were shouts and cries outside. Duncan ran to the front of the cave. The sound of guns came from the forest. There were many Indians on the other side of the river.

'Hurons!' thought Duncan.

Then Duncan saw Hawk-eye. The scout was shooting from the flat rock. Duncan saw a Huron fall into the rushing water. Then the other Hurons ran back into the forest.

Hawk-eye came back into the cave. 'They have gone,' he said.

'Will they come back?' asked Duncan.

'Yes, they will come back,' replied Hawk-eye. 'Miss Cora and Miss Alice must stay here in the cave. We will go to the rocks and wait for the Hurons.'

Duncan, Hawk-eye, Uncas and Chingachgook sat with their guns. They sat behind some rocks near the waterfall. They waited. Minutes passed. Then an hour passed.

Suddenly they heard the wild cries of the Hurons again. Four Indians ran across the flat rock towards the cave. Chingachgook and Uncas fired their guns. The first two Hurons fell to the ground. The third Huron jumped on Hawk-eye. Each man had a knife. But Hawk-eye was stronger than the Huron. He killed the Huron with his knife.

The fourth Huron fought with Duncan. Uncas ran to help the officer. The young Mohican killed the Huron. Then Uncas and Duncan ran back to the rocks.

The Hurons on the other side of the river started to shoot again. And Chingachgook shot at them.

The shooting went on and on. Rocks and trees near the cave were broken in a hundred places. But Hawk-eye and his friends were not hurt. And Cora and Alice were safe in the cave.

Hawk-eye saw a Huron in a tree on the other side of the river. The scout lifted his long gun and fired. There was a cry and the Indian fell from the tree.

'I have no more bullets,' said Hawk-eye. 'Uncas! Go to the canoe. There are some bullets in the canoe.'

Uncas ran quickly across the flat rock. But he was too late. A Huron was pushing the canoe across the river!

Duncan, Hawk-eye and the two Mohicans went back to the cave.

'What can we do now?' asked Duncan.

Hawk-eye thought for a few minutes. 'There will be guards on the paths,' he said. 'The Hurons will watch every path. We must swim. We must jump into the river. The rushing water will take us past the Hurons.'

The scout looked at Cora and Alice.

'We cannot swim,' said Cora. 'Alice and I will stay here. Go to General Munro at Fort William Henry. General Munro must send soldiers.'

Chingachgook, Uncas and Hawk-eye talked quietly together. Then Chingachgook ran out of the cave and jumped into the river. A moment later, Hawk-eye put down his long gun and followed Chingachgook. The rushing water took them away.

Cora looked at Uncas. 'Go with them,' she said.

'I will stay,' said the young Mohican.

'No!' said Cora. 'Please, Uncas. Go with them!'

Uncas was unhappy. But he jumped into the water too.

Cora looked at Duncan.

'I am going to stay,' said Duncan. He looked at Alice. 'I cannot leave you.'

———

There were shouts and cries from the Hurons on the flat rock. Duncan looked out of the cave.

The Hurons were looking behind the rocks near the waterfall.

'They are looking for us,' thought Duncan. He went quickly back into the cave.

'Our friends will bring help soon,' he said to Cora and Alice.

Cora was afraid. Her face was white. She cried out.

Duncan turned – and he saw the terrible face of Magua!

'Where are the Mohicans?' asked Magua. 'Where is the scout, Hawk-eye – The Long Gun?'

Suddenly, the cave was full of Hurons. One of them picked up Hawk-eye's gun.

'They have gone,' said Duncan. 'They will bring help soon.'

The Hurons were angry. They were going to kill their prisoners. But Magua spoke to them, quickly and quietly. Then the Hurons took Duncan, Cora and

Alice to the flat rock. One of the Hurons brought the canoe.

'Get into the canoe!' Magua said.

Duncan and the sisters got into the canoe. Magua and the Hurons took them across the river.

The prisoners got out of the canoe on the other side of the river. Magua and five Hurons stayed with them. The other Hurons walked away into the forest.

4

'I Am a Huron Chief'

The Hurons and their prisoners started to walk. Magua walked in front of Duncan, Cora and Alice. The other Hurons walked behind the prisoners. They walked across a valley. Then Magua led them up a steep hill. The land at the top of the hill was flat. Magua sat down under a tree. The Hurons started to eat and drink.

Magua shouted to Duncan. 'Send the dark-haired woman to me!'

Cora was afraid. She went to Magua. 'What do you want?' she asked.

'I am a Huron chief,' said Magua. 'I lived twenty summers and twenty winters. I did not see a white man. I was happy! Then a white man came to the forest. He gave me brandy. The drink was bad for me. It made me crazy! My people were angry. I had to go away. I ran away and lived with the Mohawks.'

'Then the war started,' said Magua. 'The French and the English were fighting each other. The Mohawks were fighting for the English. The Hurons were fighting for the French. I was fighting my own people.'

'Your father – Munro – was our chief. He told the Mohawks, "Do not drink brandy!" But a white man gave me brandy. What did Munro do? He gave orders to his men. They tied me with ropes and they beat me! I will never forget!'

'But—' said Cora.

'Woman!' shouted Magua. He stood up quickly. 'You will be my wife! Your sister will go to Fort William Henry. She must tell Munro everything. Then Munro will know. His daughter lives with me – Magua.'

'Never!' said Cora. 'I will not be your wife.'

Magua smiled. 'Then you will die,' he said. 'And your friends will die too.'

Then Magua went towards the other Hurons. He spoke to them.

Duncan ran to Cora. 'What is wrong?' he asked. 'What did Magua say to you?'

'It is not important,' said Cora.

The Hurons were listening to Magua. Duncan watched them. They were very angry. Suddenly, Magua shouted at the Hurons. They pulled Duncan and the women towards the trees. They tied each prisoner to a tree with rope.

Magua stood in front of Cora. He laughed. 'What does Munro's daughter say now?' he said. 'Shall I send your sister to your father? Will you follow me to the Great Lakes and live with me?'

Cora looked at her sister.

'Alice,' said Cora. 'I must go with Magua and be his wife. Then you and Duncan will live.'

'No!' shouted Duncan. 'Never!'

'No, no, no!' said Alice.

'Then die!' shouted Magua.

He threw his knife at Alice. The knife cut off some of her hair. It hit the tree above her head. Duncan shouted angrily.

The Hurons had tied Duncan to a tree. But he pulled the rope and it broke. He jumped on a Huron and they fought. The Huron had a knife. He was going to kill Duncan.

Suddenly a gun fired and the Huron fell dead.

5
Fort William Henry

Hawk-eye ran from the forest. Chingachgook and Uncas followed him. There was a fight. Hawk-eye, Uncas and Duncan killed four Hurons. Chingachgook jumped on Magua. The Mohican stabbed Magua with his knife. Magua fell to the ground.

Hawk-eye and Duncan went and helped the two women. But Magua was not dead. He got up and ran away. Chingachgook and Uncas ran after him.

'Stop!' shouted Hawk-eye. 'You cannot catch him.'

'Hawk-eye, how did you find us?' Duncan asked.

'We waited at the side of the river,' said Hawk-eye. 'We saw the Hurons take you across the river. Then we followed you.'

'You saved my life,' said Duncan.

Hawk-eye smiled. 'I found a Huron's gun,' he said. 'The Hurons were stupid. They left their guns under the trees.'

Hawk-eye went back to the trees. He picked up the other guns. He found his own long gun.

'Now we have guns and bullets,' he said. 'We will stay here tonight. Tomorrow we will go to Fort William Henry.'

———

Very early the next morning, Hawk-eye woke his

friends. He led them across the valley and along a path through the forest. They stopped near a small river.

'We will walk in the water,' said Hawk-eye. 'Then Magua will not see our footprints on the ground.'

They walked in the river for an hour. Then they came to some mountains.

'Walk quietly now!' said Hawk-eye. 'There are French soldiers here.'

They walked to the top of a mountain and looked down. There was Lake Horican! And there was Fort William Henry! Smoke came from fires in the forest.

'Look at the fires,' said Hawk-eye. 'There are many Hurons in the forest. They are fighting for the French.'

'And look to the west,' said Duncan. 'Look at those tents. That is General Montcalm's camp. There are thousands of French soldiers.'

Suddenly they heard the sound of guns.

'The French are shooting at Fort William Henry,' said Duncan. 'But we must get into the fort.'

'We are lucky,' said Hawk-eye. 'Thick fog is coming along the valley. The fog will hide us from the French. Follow me!'

Hawk-eye and the Mohicans started to walk down the mountain. Duncan and the two sisters followed them. At the bottom of the mountain, the fog was very thick.

'Be careful!' said Hawk-eye. 'There are many French soldiers along this path. Walk quietly!'

They followed him through the fog. Suddenly, they heard voices.

'Who is there?' said a soldier in French.

Duncan replied in French. 'A friend of France!' he said.

'Who are you?' shouted the Frenchman.

But Duncan and his friends walked away quickly. They went on through the fog. At last, they arrived at the walls of the fort.

An English voice shouted from the top of the wall. 'The French are here. Shoot! Shoot!'

'Father, Father!' Alice shouted. 'It is us! Save your

daughters!'

'Don't shoot, men!' said the voice of General Munro. 'My daughters are here! Open the gates!'

The gates opened. Soldiers came out of the fort. They took everybody inside – Duncan, the young women, Hawk-eye and the Mohicans.

But everybody in Fort William Henry was in danger.

6

'When Will Help Come?'

Days passed. The French army fired their big guns at Fort William Henry. Many English soldiers were killed. General Munro waited. But General Webb did not send any soldiers. Munro sent Hawk-eye to Fort Edward with a message.

General Webb gave Hawk-eye a letter for Munro. The scout started to go back to Fort William Henry. But French soldiers stopped him. They took the letter. They tied Hawk-eye's hands with rope.

The next morning, Duncan Heyward was standing by the gates of Fort William Henry. He saw three men coming towards the fort. He went to General Munro.

'General Munro,' he said. 'Two French soldiers are at the gates of the fort. Hawk-eye is with them. But when will help come from Fort Edward?'

Hawk-eye came into General Munro's room.

'General Webb gave me a letter for you,' he said. 'But the French soldiers took it. General Montcalm wants to speak to you. You must go to his camp.'

A French officer met Munro and Duncan at the gates of the fort. They went to General Montcalm's tent in the French camp.

There were French officers and Indian chiefs in the tent. Then Duncan saw Magua. Magua was fighting for the French! The Huron looked at Duncan and smiled.

Montcalm spoke first. He spoke to Munro.

'You have fought well, General,' he said. 'But now you must stop fighting.'

Montcalm gave a letter to Munro. Munro read it quickly. Then he gave it to Duncan. The letter was from General Webb.

we cannot send any
more men. The Indians
have killed too many
of my soldiers.

Munro looked at Duncan. They did not speak.

Then General Montcalm spoke to Munro. 'You and your soldiers must leave Fort William Henry,' he said. 'You can take your guns. But do not take your bullets. Your men, women and children will be safe. But we will burn the fort.'

General Munro was unhappy. 'We will leave in the morning,' he said. Then he and Duncan went back to the fort.

Magua was angry. He spoke to the Huron chiefs. 'The English will leave the fort. The French will not kill them. But the English are the enemies of the Hurons. We will kill the English!'

———

Three thousand English people – soldiers, women and children – left the fort. They walked past the French soldiers and they walked towards the forest. The English soldiers carried their guns. But they had no bullets.

Magua and the Hurons were standing in the forest. They watched Fort William Henry. The English left the fort and walked into the forest. Then two thousand Indians attacked!

The English could not fight. They had no bullets in their guns. Many of the English were killed.

Alice and Cora saw their father. He was running towards the French camp. He was going to find Montcalm. He was going to ask for help.

'Father! Father!' shouted Alice. 'We are here!'

But Munro did not hear them. He did not stop.

Magua was watching. He ran to Cora. 'Will you come with me now?' he said.

'Never!' said Cora. 'I will not be your wife.'

The Huron looked at her. But he did not speak. Then he turned to Alice. He held Alice's arms. He pulled her towards a horse.

'Stop!' shouted Cora. And she ran after them.

Magua put Alice on the horse. Then he put Cora on the horse too. The Huron took them along a path towards Lake Horican.

7
The Trail

Three days had passed. Fort William Henry had burnt down. The French soldiers had gone. The Indians had gone. The bodies of many English soldiers, women and children lay on the ground.

In the evening, five men walked through the forest. Munro, Duncan, Hawk-eye, Chingachgook and Uncas were looking for Cora and Alice. They found the dead bodies of many English people. The five men were sad and angry.

Suddenly, Uncas shouted to the others, 'Look!'

He had a small piece of cloth in his hand.

'That is a piece of Cora's dress!' said Munro.

Uncas found footprints on the ground, near a tree.

'Three people and a horse have stood here,' he said.

Then Chingachgook found Alice's necklace. And he found another piece of Cora's dress.

Duncan took the necklace. He smiled. 'Alice is alive,' he said.

'Miss Cora has left a trail,' said Hawk-eye. 'She has left pieces of her dress. We can follow this trail. But we must go quietly. Magua is with them.'

'But it is late,' said Hawk-eye. 'We will eat some food. We will sleep here tonight. Tomorrow we will follow Miss Cora's trail.'

———

Very early the next morning, Hawk-eye woke the English officers and the Mohicans.

The five men followed Cora's trail. It led them to Lake Horican. Uncas and Chingachgook found a canoe in the grass near the lake.

The five men got into the canoe. The Mohicans paddled it along the lake.

After half an hour, Uncas spoke quietly.

'Smoke,' he said. He was looking at a small island in front of them.

'Smoke from a fire,' said Hawk-eye. 'And there are two canoes.'

Suddenly, some Hurons ran from the trees on the island. They got into the two canoes.

'They are following us,' said Duncan. 'Paddle faster!'

'No! Stop paddling, Chingachgook,' said Hawk-eye. 'I will shoot them.' And he lifted his long gun.

He fired. A Huron in the first canoe fell into the lake. The Hurons stopped their two canoes. They did not follow.

Chingachgook and Uncas started paddling again. The five men went on. They went north, up the lake.

8

The Medicine Man

In the evening, the five men arrived at the north end of Lake Horican. They got out of the canoe and Uncas and Chingachgook carried it. They put it under some trees.

'We have lost the trail,' said Duncan. 'Where shall we go?'

'My Mohican friends know the path to the Hurons' village,' said Hawk-eye. 'It is north of this place. That is where Magua is going. We will go north too.'

———

For two days, the men followed the path. They walked many miles. They arrived at the Hurons' village on the second day. It was early evening. There were about a hundred houses by a small lake.

Hawk-eye spoke to Chingachgook and Uncas. Then he spoke to Duncan and Munro.

'General Munro, stay with Chingachgook,' said Hawk-eye. 'Stay in the forest. Duncan and I will go into the village. Uncas, go up the hill to the west. Watch the village. Come back quickly. Tell us about the guards.'

An hour passed. The four men waited. Uncas did not come back.

Suddenly Duncan spoke. 'I have a plan,' he said. 'Hawk-eye, give me your coat. I must not wear my red soldier's coat in the village. I will be a medicine man – a French doctor. I will speak French. I will walk through the village and go into the houses. The Hurons will not hurt a medicine man. I will find Alice and Cora.'

It was a dangerous plan.

Duncan put on Hawk-eye's coat. Then he walked into the Hurons' village. There was a large wooden building in front of him. It was the meeting-house of the Huron chiefs. Duncan went inside.

Some Huron chiefs were sitting together. They saw Duncan come in. One of the chiefs walked forward. His hair was grey and he was tall and strong. He spoke to Duncan in the Huron language. But Duncan did not understand.

'Do you speak French?' Duncan asked.

The Huron replied in French. 'Why are you here?' he asked.

'I am a medicine man,' said Duncan. 'The King of France sent me. Are any Hurons ill?'

Suddenly, there were loud cries from the forest. The chiefs left the meeting-house. Duncan followed them. More Hurons were coming into the village. There was a prisoner in front of them. It was Uncas!

9

In the Hurons' Village

Uncas was not afraid. The Hurons ran around him. They shouted. They pulled him towards the wooden building. Uncas saw Duncan outside the building.

'Hawk-eye is safe, Uncas,' Duncan said quietly. Then the Hurons took Uncas into the meeting-house.

Duncan walked through the village. He looked in the houses. Nobody stopped him. Nobody asked any questions. But Duncan did not find Alice and Cora.

He went back to the meeting-house. He went inside. Uncas was standing and the chiefs were sitting. Duncan sat down too. He sat near the wall.

Then another Huron came into the building. It was Magua! Magua did not see Duncan. But he saw Uncas. He shouted, 'Mohican, you must die!'

Magua was angry. He turned to the chiefs. 'Many Hurons died at Glenn's Falls,' he said. 'This Mohican is our enemy!'

Magua and two Hurons took the young Mohican out of the meeting-house.

Then one of the chiefs spoke to Duncan. 'Medicine man, the wife of one of my men is ill – she is sick. Can you make her well?'

'Take me to the woman,' said Duncan.

He followed the chief out of the meeting-house. They went towards a hill. There was a cave in the hill.

Duncan saw a bear following them. But he was not afraid. Indians liked bears. They often had bears in their villages.

Duncan followed the chief into the cave. The cave was large and there were many rooms with stone walls. The chief took Duncan into one room. The sick woman was lying on the ground. Some other women were with her. Duncan looked at the sick woman. 'She is dying,' he thought.

The Huron chief waited and looked at Duncan.

Duncan turned to the Huron chief. 'I must look at this sick woman alone,' he said. 'My medicine is secret. Go with these four women. Wait outside.'

The chief and the four women left the cave.

A few minutes later, the bear came into the cave. The bear made a loud noise. Duncan looked at the bear. Again, the bear made a loud noise. It walked towards Duncan. Suddenly, it took off its head! It was Hawk-eye! Hawk-eye was wearing a bear's skin!

'What—?' said Duncan. Then he laughed. 'Why are you wearing a bear's skin?' he asked.

'I found the bear's skin in a Huron's house,' said Hawk-eye. 'Now the Hurons will not stop me. But tell me. Where is Miss Alice?'

'I have been unlucky. I have not found Alice or Cora. And Uncas is a prisoner of the Hurons.'

'Magua has taken Miss Cora to the village of the Delawares,' said Hawk-eye. 'I heard two Hurons talking about her. Chingachgook and Munro are safe in the forest.'

Then Hawk-eye heard a noise. He looked over a stone wall. 'Miss Alice is in the next room!' he said.

Duncan went into the next room. There were some blankets, cloths and animals' skins in the room. And there was Alice. Her hands and feet were tied with rope. Her face was white. She was afraid.

'Duncan!' she said. 'You are here.'

'Yes,' said Duncan. He untied her hands and feet.

'Where is Cora?' asked Alice. 'Where is my father?'

'Your father is safe. He is with Chingachgook,' said Duncan.

'And Cora?' Alice asked again.

'She is near here. She is at another village,' said Duncan. 'She is with the Delawares.'

Suddenly, somebody came into the room. It was Magua!

10

The Bear

Magua looked at Duncan and Alice. He laughed and went towards them. Suddenly the bear was in the room. It quickly held Magua. Magua could not move. He could not turn round.

Duncan ran to the Huron. He tied Magua's arms. Then he tied Magua's feet. Magua started to speak, but Duncan put a cloth into his mouth.

Hawk-eye took off the bear's head. 'We must go quickly,' he said. 'Alice, you will wear a blanket. You will be the sick Huron woman. Then you can leave the Hurons' village.'

Hawk-eye put on the bear's head again. Alice put a blanket over her head. Duncan carried Alice out of the cave. And Hawk-eye followed Duncan.

The Huron chief was outside the cave.

'I am taking the sick woman away,' said Duncan. 'I will bring her to your house tomorrow.'

Hawk-eye, Duncan and Alice left the village. Then Hawk-eye led Duncan and Alice to a path.

'This path goes to a small river,' Hawk-eye said to them. 'You will see a hill. The village of the Delawares is near the hill. You will be safe with the Delawares.'

'What are you going to do?' asked Duncan.

'I must go back for Uncas,' said Hawk-eye.

It was dark in the village. The Hurons were in their houses. They were asleep. Hawk-eye was looking for Uncas. The scout was wearing the bear's skin. He looked in all the buildings. Then he saw two men outside a house. They were guards. But they were asleep. Hawk-eye quietly went inside the house.

Uncas was lying on the floor. His hands and feet were tied with rope. Hawk-eye took off the bear's head. Uncas smiled.

'Hawk-eye,' he said quietly.

Hawk-eye untied Uncas' hands and feet. Then he took off the bear's skin. Uncas and Hawk-eye ran quickly from the village.

'We shall go to the Delawares' village,' said Hawk-eye.

'Yes!' said Uncas. 'The Delawares are the children of my grandfather. They will help us.'

———

The next morning, the Hurons went to get Uncas. They were going to kill him. They found the bear's skin. But they did not find the Mohican.

Then they went to the cave. They found a dead woman. But they did not find Alice.

They found Magua. His hands and feet were tied. A cloth was in his mouth.

The Hurons untied Magua's hands and feet. They took the cloth from his mouth.

Magua was angry. 'Kill the Mohican prisoner now!' he shouted.

'He has gone,' said one of the chiefs.

Magua shouted with anger. And he ran out of the cave.

11

The Old Chief

Magua went to the Delawares' village. The Delawares were friends of France. But they did not fight in the war.

Magua went to the Delawares' meeting-house. The Delaware chiefs were talking.

'The Huron chief is welcome,' said a Delaware.

'Is my woman prisoner safe and well?' asked Magua.

'She is well,' said the Delaware.

Then Magua said, 'Are there strangers in the forest? White men?'

'There are strangers in the village,' said the Delaware. 'They are in my house. But strangers are always welcome in this village.'

'What will the King of France say about this?' said Magua. 'His greatest enemy is here in the Delawares' village. This enemy is a white man. He kills many friends of the French.'

'Which white man is an enemy of France?' asked the Delaware chief.

'The scout, Hawk-eye!' said Magua. 'The Long Gun! The other strangers are his friends. They are the enemies of France too.'

The Delawares started to talk quietly. One of them left the meeting-house quickly. A few minutes later, he came back.

Then a very old man came into the meeting-house. Two young Delawares helped the old man. He had long white hair and there were many lines on his face. The chiefs spoke his name – 'Tamenund.'

Magua knew the name of this famous Delaware chief. Tamenund was more than one hundred years old!

Tamenund sat down. Then he spoke to the two young Delawares. They got up and went away.

Soon, they came back with Alice, Cora, Duncan and Hawk-eye.

Cora was very angry. She spoke to the chiefs.

'Yesterday, we were welcome in this village,' she said. 'The Delawares were our friends. Today we are your prisoners. Why are we prisoners?'

Tamenund did not answer.

'Which man is Hawk-eye, The Long Gun?' he asked.

Hawk-eye walked forward. 'I am Hawk-eye,' he said.

Then Tamenund spoke quickly to Magua.

'Take your prisoner – the dark-haired woman. Go!' he said.

But Cora spoke to the old chief.

'Another man came to this village with us,' she said. 'Now he is a prisoner too. But he is one of your own people. He will tell our story. Please! Listen to him!'

Tamenund looked at the chiefs. 'Who is this other prisoner?' he asked.

'He fights for the English,' Magua said quickly. 'You must kill him.'

'Bring him here!' said Tamenund.

Two men left the meeting-house. Soon they came back with Uncas.

Uncas was not wearing a shirt. His hands were tied. He stood in front of Tamenund. The old chief looked at him. Tamenund saw a tattoo on Uncas' chest. It was a picture of a turtle.

Tamenund looked at Uncas. Then he smiled at the young Mohican. 'Your father is a great chief,' he said.

Uncas suddenly saw Hawk-eye. 'Delaware Father,' he said to Tamenund. 'This is my friend, Hawk-eye. He is a friend of the Delawares.'

'The Long Gun?' said Tamenund. 'He is not a friend of the Delawares. He kills our young men.'

Then Hawk-eye spoke. 'I kill Hurons,' he said. 'I have never killed a Delaware.'

The Delawares believed Hawk-eye's words.

Tamenund looked at Uncas. 'Why are you the Huron's prisoner?' he asked.

'I helped the English woman,' said Uncas.

Tamenund looked at Cora. Then he spoke to Magua.

'And why is the English woman your prisoner?' he asked.

'I hate the English!' said Magua. 'Now the daughter of an English chief is my prisoner. Now the daughter of Munro will be my wife.'

Magua went to Cora and held her arm.

'Wait!' shouted Duncan. 'Don't take her. The English will give you money.'

But Magua did not listen. He pulled Cora towards the door. 'Come!' he said to her.

'I am your prisoner,' Cora said to Magua. 'But do not touch me.'

She turned to Duncan. 'Please take care of my young sister,' she said. She kissed Alice.

Then she spoke to Magua. 'I will come with you.'

'And I will come too!' shouted Duncan. 'I will help you, Cora!'

'Wait!' said Hawk-eye. He held Duncan's arm. Hawk-eye spoke quickly and quietly.

'Magua's friends are waiting in the forest,' he said. 'They will kill you.'

'Huron!' said Uncas. 'We will find you! We will kill you!'

But Magua laughed. 'Mohican,' said Magua. 'you cannot kill me. I am too strong. Stay here with your brothers, the Delawares. They are weak. They like their homes and their food. They do not like fighting. They will not help you.'

Then Magua walked out of the meeting-house. Cora followed him.

Uncas spoke to Tamenund. 'Delaware Father,' he said. 'Help us. We must follow the English woman.'

Tamenund called the young men of the village. 'Go with the Mohican,' he said. 'The Hurons are now our enemies!'

12

The Last of the Mohicans

Magua and Cora walked into the forest. They walked towards the Hurons' village.

An hour later, Hawk-eye, Duncan and Uncas followed Magua's trail. Two hundred young Delawares went with the three friends. Alice stayed in the Delawares' village.

Hawk-eye spoke to Uncas.

'Major Heyward and I will find Chingachgook and General Munro,' he said. 'They are safe in the forest. Uncas, take the Delawares with you. Follow Magua's trail. Be careful! There will be many Hurons in the forest. We will meet you at the Hurons' village.'

'Magua will take Cora to the cave in the hill,' said Hawk-eye. 'We will find her! We will help her!'

'Come,' said Duncan.

———

Hawk-eye and Duncan soon found Chingachgook and Munro. They quickly told Munro their story. Then the four men went to the Hurons' village. They walked up the hill towards the cave.

Suddenly, they heard shouts and cries. They looked down at the village. Uncas and the Delawares were fighting the Hurons in the village. Then Magua and some Hurons ran up the hill. They were going to the cave. Uncas was running after them. Hawk-eye and his friends fought the Hurons. The fight was terrible, but Magua escaped.

Then Hawk-eye, Duncan, Munro, the Mohicans and their friends saw Magua again. He was with another Huron. They were in front of the cave. The two Indians were pulling Cora from the cave.

'Cora!' shouted Duncan. 'There is Cora!'

Uncas ran towards the rocks above the cave. Cora had stopped in front of the cave.

Magua took out his knife. He turned to Cora.

'Woman!' he shouted. 'Will you be the wife of Magua? Or will you die?'

'Kill me, Magua!' Cora said. 'I will not go with you!'

Suddenly there was a cry. Uncas was standing on the rocks above them. Magua looked up. The other Huron turned to Cora. He stabbed her with his knife and killed her.

Magua shouted angrily. He lifted his knife and killed the Huron. Then Uncas jumped on Magua. They fought. But Magua turned quickly. He stabbed Uncas four times. The young Mohican stood for a moment. Then he fell at Magua's feet – dead.

Hawk-eye saw Uncas fall. The scout ran towards Magua. Magua ran up the path. His enemies were below him. Magua climbed up the rocks. Then he turned and looked down.

Hawk-eye stopped running. He lifted his long gun. Magua jumped towards a higher rock and Hawk-eye fired. Magua's fingers touched the rock. But the bullet from Hawk-eye's gun killed him. And his body fell down and down onto the rocks.

A day later, General Munro, Duncan and Alice stood by the graves of Uncas and Cora. They were sad and silent. Then they said goodbye to Hawk-eye, Chingachgook, and the Delawares. And they walked away into the forest.

Chingachgook looked at Hawk-eye. 'All the people of my tribe have gone now,' he said. 'I am alone.'

'No,' said Hawk-eye. 'Uncas has gone. But you are not alone.' He put his hand on Chingachgook's hand.

The tears of the two friends fell onto the grave of Uncas.

———

In 1758, General Munro died. Alice married Duncan Heyward and they lived happily together.

From that time, the Delawares told their children the story of the English woman and the young Mohican. And they told their children the words of Tamenund, the old chief –

'The time of the red man has gone. We fought for our land. But now there are many white men – as many as the leaves on the trees. I have lived too long. I have seen the last of the Mohicans!'

Published by Macmillan Heinemann ELT
Between Towns Road, Oxford, OX4 3PP
Macmillan Heinemann ELT is an imprint of
Macmillan Publishers Limited

Companies and representatives throughout the world

ISBN 0 435 27338 8

Heinemann is a registered trade mark of Reed Educational & Professional Publishing Ltd

This retold version for Macmillan Guided Readers
Text © John Escott, 1997 ,2002
Design and illustration © Macmillan Publishers Limited 1998, 2002
This version first published 2002

Acknowledgement: The publishers would like to thank Popperfoto
for permission to reproduce the picture on page 4.

Illustrated by Annabel Large. Map on page 3, by John Gilkes
Cover by David Bull and Marketplace Design

Printed in China

2006 2005 2004 2003 2002
15 14 13 12 11 10 9 8 7 6